Y0-BEC-003

MYSTERY IN THE APPLE ORCHARD

Mystery in the Apple Orchard

By

HELEN FULLER ORTON

ILLUSTRATED BY ROBERT DOREMUS

J. B. Lippincott Company
Philadelphia & New York

CONTENTS

1	Morning in the Orchard	page	1
2	A Ribbon Vanishes		13
3	Gloria Wears Her Diamond		24
4	The Airplane Game		35
5	"It's Gone!"		49
6	A Frantic Search		58
7	Mr. Crow's Nest		68
8	Chippie's House		77
9	A Light in the Orchard		88
10	Timmy Climbs a Tree		96
11	The Mystery in the Orchard		106

MYSTERY IN THE APPLE ORCHARD

CHAPTER ONE

Morning in the Orchard

ON A SATURDAY morning in spring, Dee Waters sighed with satisfaction as she finished her homework for Monday. Then she skipped out through the big old-fashioned kitchen to the side porch to see what the weather was going to be.

"It isn't going to rain after all," she said. "There's a rift in the clouds, Mother. We can play in the old orchard today, can't we?"

Mrs. Waters stepped to the door and studied the sky. "Yes, it's going to be a pleasant day. Have a good time in the apple trees."

She gave Dee's short brown curls an affectionate pat.

"Oh, I will," Dee assured her. "I always do. But I love it best when the trees are in bloom."

Mother gazed out across the orchard. "What can be prettier than an orchard in bloom?" she asked. "I wish I had time to spend the day with you looking at the blossoms and listening to the birds."

"I wish you had!" Dee said, hugging her mother. Then, "Where's Ronnie?" she asked.

"He's already out there," Mother told her, smiling. "He skipped out right after breakfast."

"I think I'll make a couple of sandwiches. We might get hungry before noon," Dee said, returning to the kitchen.

"Good idea," Mother agreed. "There's peanut butter and strawberry jam in the pantry. Help yourself, dear."

Dee spread the peanut butter and jam generously on the bread slices. She wrapped each sandwich in aluminum foil and put the two together and tied them with a blue ribbon. She ran back to her room and slipped into her sneakers. The rubber soles made tree climbing so much easier! Then she selected a book to read. This and the sandwiches she fitted into a small basket and, swinging it over her arm, hurried outdoors.

2

"Good-by!" she called to her mother. "If you want me for anything, just call. I can hear you from anywhere in the orchard."

She ran down the steps, then across the side yard and along a path through the garden. Beyond the garden there was an old stone well. Years ago it had supplied drinking water for the house. But now it was filled to the brim with earth and stones. A bed of spearmint had grown up around the stones. Dee stopped and picked a spicy sprig and chewed it as she hurried on.

When she came to the first tree, she reached to a spray of the pink-and-white blossoms, but she pulled her hand back.

"No, I won't pick them," she decided. "They are so pretty there on the tree. Besides, some of them may grow into nice juicy apples by fall."

This was a very old orchard. It had been planted by Grandfather Waters, who was experimenting with apples. Each tree was a different kind. The children knew the names of all the varieties, for their father had taught them what they were.

The limbs of the trees were large and strong. All winter long the branches had been bare and brown, but now on each little twig there was a cluster of pink blossoms. The whole orchard was like one big bouquet.

Father had never had the ground plowed, so the sod was soft and thick under the trees. Dee walked along till she came to her favorite Harvest-Apple tree, with its wide-spreading branches that were low enough to be within her reach.

"I wonder where Ronnie is?" she thought.

4

She glanced around among the trees and called her brother's name. There was no answer.

"He must be somewhere else," she decided. "I'll sit up here on the lower limb and read to myself till he comes back."

But it wasn't easy to keep her mind on the story when there were so many interesting things going on around her. A bluebird was singing in the top of the tree. A busy-looking robin hopped over the grass, searching for worms. A squirrel scurried up the trunk of the next tree and ducked into a deep hollow in the side of it.

Unexpectedly Dee heard a laugh coming from the top of her tree. A boy's voice teased, "Couldn't see me! Couldn't find me! And I was here all the time."

"My goodness! Where are you?" Dee asked, craning her neck.

"Right here! Come on up."

She saw her brother's bright shirt high among the branches.

"All right. I will. Wait till I put my book and basket away."

She reached over and hung her basket on a nearby branch. Then she scrambled up over the fat branches until she was perched on a limb below Ronnie.

"See! I can climb, too!" she cried triumphantly. "Even though I'm only nine and a half to your eleven. Oh, how pretty everything looks from here!"

Ronnie nodded. "And you can see so far, too. I've been watching the telephone men string new wire along our road. You should see them climb! Lickety-split and they're at the top of the pole."

Dee stretched way up so she, too, could see the road. "Yes. There they are," she said. "But I'd rather look at our apple trees. Aren't we lucky to have such a wonderful orchard to play in?"

"We sure are," Ronnie agreed. "I feel sorry for city kids."

"Me, too," Dee said. "Oh, look!"

Below, a tiny animal with dark brown and white stripes along his brownish back was frisking about in nervous leaps.

"A ground squirrel," Ronnie said.

"A chipmunk!" Dee exclaimed.

She reached into her pocket and brought out a crushed cooky. She threw the crumbs on the ground.

Chippy's bright eyes spied the crumbs. He darted

toward them. In a wink he had gobbled them up, stuffing them into the pouches in his cheeks. He jumped back a few feet, then sat up on his little haunches and stared up at Dee, as if to say, "I hope you have more of those good things for me."

"With his little cheeks so full, he looks as if he had the mumps." Dee laughed softly.

She began to inch down toward her basket. When she could reach it, she pulled out the sandwiches. As she untied the blue ribbon, it slipped from her fingers and sailed down into a patch of violets under the tree.

"I must be sure to get it when I go down," she said. "It's too pretty to lose."

She unfolded the aluminum foil and a crumpled bit of it broke off and fell to the ground near the ribbon. Then she tore off the crust from one of the sandwiches and tossed it over toward Chippy. He grabbed it and ran off to another tree. Dee watched as he disappeared into the sod and hauled the crust in after him with a determined yank.

"Well, of all things!" she exclaimed. "Do you suppose Chippy lives down there? I'm going down to see."

7

"You go ahead," Ronnie said. "But leave me the sandwiches. I'm hungry."

"All right."

Her brother swung down to a lower branch and Dee handed him the sandwiches.

"You may have them both," she said. "I don't want any."

"Thanks!" Ronnie said, promptly sinking his teeth into the one spread with jam.

Dee took her basket and slid down from the tree and ran over to the spot where the chipmunk had vanished in the ground.

"There's a tiny hole here," she said. "That must be Chippy's front door. But how could he get down through such a small opening?"

"He's not very big himself," Ronnie pointed out, his mouth rather full. "Chipmunks always have little doors like that. He probably has another one, for safety's sake, six or seven feet away. Chippies are smart."

"I don't want him afraid of me," Dee said, going back to the tree.

She did not climb up this time, however. Taking her book from the basket she leaned against the trunk and leafed through the pages. But soon a squirrel

8

with a long fluffy tail, which he kept arched, came hopping along.

"A gray squirrel!" Dee said softly. "And what do you want?"

She made a motion with her hand as she said this, and it so frightened the small creature that he flicked his tail and was gone in a flash up another tree. He scooted up the trunk and vanished into a large hollow.

"I'll never get a chapter read today," Dee declared. "Not with all these animals running around. My book report will have to wait."

She returned her book to the basket, on top of the folded aluminum sandwich sheet, and set the basket carefully on a patch of clover. As she straightened up, a girl's voice floated over the fence that ran along the road side of the orchard.

"Dee-ee! Dee-ee!"

"There's Emily Harris!" Dee announced, and called back, "Over here, Emily. Come on over. We're at the Harvest-Apple tree."

A dark-haired girl of about Dee's age ducked under the fence and ran swiftly across the grass, her short pigtails bobbing.

"We've been watching the animals in the orchard,"

Dee told her friend. "Let's sit quietly and maybe some of them will come back."

Emily settled herself on the grass near Dee. Sure enough, the bold little chipmunk was soon back, watching them with bright beady eyes.

But Ronnie directed their attention elsewhere.

"There's a big crow," he whispered from his perch.

He pointed to the ground under another tree. A crow had alighted and was walking toward the crumpled bit of shiny aluminum foil Dee had dropped earlier. The breeze had carried it away from the Harvest-Apple. Now it sparkled like a diamond in the sun.

"Be quiet, girls, and don't move, so we can see what he's going to do," Ronnie said.

The crow would walk a few feet, then stop and glance around cautiously, as if afraid he was being followed. He was funny, and the girls covered their mouths to keep from giggling out loud. But Mr. Crow kept getting closer and closer to the sparkling bit of aluminum foil.

"Hurry up, Mr. Crow!" urged Dee softly. "Show us what you're up to."

In a moment the crow picked up the piece of foil

10

in his beak and flew up through an open space between the trees. Up, up he flew toward the top of the tall walnut tree at the south side of the orchard.

"I'll bet he's going to take that piece of aluminum foil to his nest," Ronnie said. "There's a crow's nest in the top of that tree. It must be his!"

He dropped to the ground and ran across the orchard to the tall walnut. Sure enough, the big bird flapped to the top of it and alighted on the topmost branches. Then he jumped down to the edge of the rough nest that could be seen in the crotch between one of the limbs and the trunk of the tree.

Ronnie watched until Mr. Crow flapped away again without the piece of foil in his beak, then Ronnie ran back to the girls.

"Mr. Crow took that shiny foil and dropped it in his nest," he reported. "I didn't really see him drop it there, but when he flew away he didn't have it. He must like shiny things."

"That is the place to look if we lose anything like that here," Dee remarked. "We must remember."

"I wish I could look there right now. But it's too high to climb to—even for me," Ronnie said, eyeing the tall walnut regretfully.

"Sh-sh!" Emily whispered. "A squirrel's just come down from his tree."

They all watched, quiet as mice, to see what the squirrel was going to do. He was scratching in the grass not far away, his little paws digging swiftly into the sod.

"He's dug something out of the ground," Dee observed. "See, he's holding it in his paws."

"It's a hickory nut," Ronnie told them. "Probably he buried some there last fall."

The squirrel took the nut in his teeth and hurried away in long hopping arcs to the pippin tree nearby. He ran up the trunk and dove into his nest.

"Well, well. We certainly have had quite a show this morning," Ronnie remarked. "Things do happen even in a quiet orchard."

"If we lose something here," Dee said, "We can be sure one of these creatures has made off with it."

"They must have a thousand hiding places all through the garden and orchard. You'd have a fine time finding it again," Ronnie scoffed. "My advice to you, girls, is don't lose anything here!"

CHAPTER TWO

A Ribbon Vanishes

EMILY AND DEE had been sitting too long. They jumped to their feet. Emily reached up and broke off a cluster of apple blossoms and touched them to her cheek.

"They're so soft and silky cool," she said. "And such a marvelous smell. Sometimes I think apple blossoms are my favorite flowers."

Ronnie swung up into the Harvest-Apple tree again and called down to the girls, "Tell me how many petals an apple blossom has. I'll bet you can't do it without looking now."

"Four," Emily said quickly.

"Wrong."

"Six?" Dee guessed.

"Wrong again."

"It must be five then," Emily decided.

"Right."

"Does an apple blossom always have five petals?" she asked. "Doesn't it sometimes forget how many to grow and have three or four or six?"

"Always five," Ronnie said. "At least, most always. Maybe once in a million times it may forget and grow only four, I s'pose."

"How do you know so much?" Emily asked.

"I have a nature book. But I also have two eyes. You can learn a lot of interesting things if you use your eyes."

Suddenly Dee whispered, "Hush! Here's a robin that wants something."

The bird had flown down from a nearby tree and was hopping around, chirping excitedly.

"Maybe she has a nest in this tree and wishes we'd go away," Dee suggested. "Let's go and swing for a while."

"I'd love it," Emily replied.

The girls raced to the swing Mr. Waters had hung from a sturdy limb of the Baldwin tree. But Ronnie

beat them to it by dropping to the ground from a low branch ahead of them and sprinting to the swing.

"You may have the first swing, Emily," Dee said quickly when her brother made a motion of getting on himself. "Because you're a guest."

"I'll push you," Ronnie offered, wrinkling his nose at his sister. "That's what I meant to do."

His look said to Dee, "I remember my manners, too, miss!"

"I love to swing," Emily said, wriggling onto the seat.

Ronnie gave her a push and soon she was flying through the air, up, up toward the treetops.

"Oooh!" she called breathlessly. "This is grand."

She began to sing, and Dee and Ronnie joined her in the tune they all loved, *Swinging 'Neath the Old Apple Tree.*

> "Oh, the sports of childhood!
> Roaming through the wildwood,
> Running o'er the meadow,
>   Happy and free;
> But my heart's a-beating
> For the old-time greeting
> Swinging 'neath the old apple tree.

Swinging, swinging, swinging, swinging,
Lulling care to rest 'neath the old apple tree;
Swinging, swinging, swinging, swinging
Swinging 'neath the old apple tree.

Swaying in the sunbeams,
Floating in the shadow,
Sailing on the breezes,
   Happy and free;
Chasing all our sadness,
Shouting in our gladness,
Swinging 'neath the old apple tree."

"This is fun," Emily called out at the end of the song. "But I guess it's your turn now, Dee. Let the old cat die, please."

Slower and slower went the swing, until it stopped altogether, dead still.

"That was wonderful," Emily said, sliding off.

"I'll swing you, Dee," Ronnie offered. "But then it will be my turn. I don't want anyone to push me. I can swing myself."

Dee had her swing, and then Ronnie had to show the girls how high he could go by himself. He stood on the seat and sailed higher and higher in the air, until Dee screamed for him to stop.

"It's lunchtime, anyway," she shouted up to him, "so you'd better let the cat die, and fast."

"Oh, all right," Ronnie said. "But that's what I call swinging!"

"I have to go home, too," Emily said. "I think I heard my mother calling. 'By now. See you later."

She ran off, and Dee and Ronnie raced up the path toward their house. Suddenly Dee remembered something.

"I forgot the basket with my book—and my ribbon, too. I must get them."

She raced back through the trees and retrieved the basket. But the ribbon which had dropped on the patch of violets was nowhere to be seen.

"Ronnie, help me find my ribbon!" she called to her brother. "The one I had around our sandwiches."

"What's so important about a piece of ribbon? Come on home. I'm starved! Your sandwiches nowhere near filled me up, especially after all that swinging."

"But it was such a pretty blue ribbon," Dee wailed. "With gold stripes. I wanted it for my doll."

Reluctantly Ronnie joined her in the search. "If this is where you left it," he said, "it certainly isn't here now. So forget it."

"Oh-h, all right. But it didn't walk away by itself.

Do you suppose Chippie took it down to his house?
Or Mr. Crow up to his nest?"

"Could be," Ronnie said. "Could be," and dashed
away up the path, with Dee following more slowly.

Mrs. Waters had the children's lunch ready on a
table near a sunny window in the big kitchen by the
time they returned to the house. And Mrs. Brown,
who came out on a bus from the city to help their
mother with the housework, was polishing the table
top in the dining room. She was a pleasant person,
and the children liked her.

"Hello, Mrs. Brown!" they sang out when they
saw her.

"Hello, Dee! Hello, Ronnie! Isn't it a lovely
day?"

"Yes. We hated to leave the orchard," Dee said.

While they were washing their hands at the kitchen
sink, Mrs. Waters said, "We'd just about given you
two up. We thought you'd decided to stay in the
orchard and live on apple blossoms."

"Not me!" Ronnie laughed. "Not when lunch
smells so good. Come on, Dee, sit down before I
starve to death. You know what Dee did, Mother?

She fed those beautiful sandwiches she brought with her to the chipmunks and squirrels and robins and crows!"

"I did not!" Dee denied. "He's making it all up. I only fed a bit of crust to the chipmunk and Ronnie ate all the rest. The orchard is full of such wonderful creatures. I love it," Dee burbled happily.

"You children are certainly lucky to have such a wonderful place to play," Mrs. Brown said wistfully. "Fresh air and sunshine, and a nice safe orchard. Not like my Timmy."

"What's the matter with Timmy?" Dee asked, looking up from her chicken soup.

"My little boy isn't very strong," Mrs. Brown said. "He had an accident and was in the hospital for a long time. Now the doctor says he must have lots of sun and air, but in the city the only place he can get those is on the street. There aren't any trees or parks where we live."

Dee and Ronnie exchanged a long look. Mrs. Brown seldom spoke of her own troubles or of her little boy. In fact, they had forgotten she had one. Now, suddenly, he seemed very real to the brother and sister. They glanced at their mother. Mrs. Waters was looking at them, saying something with her eyes.

All at once Dee knew what it was!

"Mrs. Brown," she said, "why don't you bring Timmy out here with you when you come? We'd love to have him play with us in the orchard."

"Deary me!" Mrs. Brown gasped. "I didn't mean to—I—" Her kind eyes filled with tears.

Dee pushed away from the table and ran to her. She put her arms around Mrs. Brown. "Do please bring Timmy. It will be such fun to show him the orchard and introduce him to Chippie and Mr. Crow and the squirrels and the robins. We'll have such fun!"

"Yes, do bring him," Mrs. Waters urged. "You can see the children really want him."

"I will then. I will, indeed," Mrs. Brown promised.

Later, when Mrs. Brown had gone to work upstairs, Mrs. Waters looked at Ronnie and Dee affectionately. "I'm glad you invited Timmy to come here," she said. "But you must remember not to play roughly with him, or expect him to climb trees the way you do. Timmy has to walk with a crutch. You see, he had a very bad fall about a year ago and now he is lame. It may be a long time before he can run and play as you do."

"How did he fall?" Dee asked, her eyes big with sympathy.

"It's not a pleasant story," Mother said. "There are some mean boys in Mrs. Brown's neighborhood. They teased Timmy into climbing a tall laundry pole back of the apartment house where they live. It was made of an old telephone pole, with those metal hooks in it that linesmen climb on. Timmy climbed up, but then he became frightened and dizzy and fell to the hard concrete below. It's a wonder he lived at all. So you see why you must not expect him to climb trees, don't you?"

"Of course!" Ronnie and Dee spoke together.

"I'd like to get at those boys!" Ronnie said, his fists clenched.

Mother stroked his head. "You can't do that. But you can be nice to Timmy and make him feel welcome here."

"We'll do that all right!" brother and sister promised.

CHAPTER THREE

Gloria Wears Her Diamond

THAT WAS HOW it happened that two days later, when Dee and Ronnie and Emily came to the orchard after school, they found a boy sitting under the greening tree. He was younger than they, small and rather thin and pale. A crutch lay on the grass beside him. At this moment he was happily watching a squirrel bounding over the orchard sod.

"That's Timmy Brown," Dee whispered to Emily. "You know, the boy we told you about. We're all going to be extra nice to him and make him feel welcome. See what Ronnie made?"

Dee pointed to a carefully lettered sign nailed to a tree. On a large piece of daffodil-yellow cardboard Ronnie had printed in green capital letters:

WELCOME TO OUR ORCHARD!

Emily nodded, and the children raced over to Timmy.

"Hello, Timmy!" they called.

The small boy struggled to his feet and regarded the children shyly. "Hello," he said in a low voice. "I wasn't sure you'd really want me here until I saw your sign."

"Of course we want you!" Dee said quickly.

"How do you like our orchard?" Ronnie wanted to know.

"It's swell. I've never seen anything so pretty."

There was a rustle in the grass and a rabbit popped out and took off across the orchard toward a mound over by the south side.

Timmy's eyes were round with amazement.

"Do real live animals come close to you here all the time?" he asked. "I never saw a rabbit before except in a picture book."

"You'll see lots of animals here," Ronnie told him.

"If you're quiet and watch, maybe Chippie will come and sit beside you, or Mr. Crow will flap down to the grass, or a whole family of squirrels."

"Robins and woodpeckers, too," Dee added. "And bluebirds. All sorts of creatures."

Timmy's eyes, large in a thin little face, shone with pleasure.

A high clear whistle drew the children's attention away from their guest.

"That's Arthur Mills," Ronnie said. "Come on over, Art!"

Arthur waved and ran across the orchard toward them.

"Now that there are enough of us, let's play hide-and-seek," Ronnie proposed and was instantly sorry. Timmy could not take part in a game that required running.

"Hi!" Arthur shouted and turned a handspring. "This sure is a nice day." Then he noticed the new boy.

"This is Timmy Brown," Dee said. "He's come out from the city to play in our orchard."

"Hello," Arthur said cheerfully. He turned to Ronnie. "What's up for today?"

Ronnie hesitated before answering. "We were going to play hide-and-seek, but—"

"Don't stop on account of me," Timmy said. "I'd just as soon sit right here and watch the birds and animals."

"All right," Ronnie agreed. "If you're sure you don't mind."

Timmy shook his head. "If I get tired of sitting here, I can play marbles. Could I put them on that board over there?" He pointed to a low platform on which apples would be placed when picking time came.

"Oh sure," Ronnie said. "Help yourself."

This settled, the others were ready for their game. They counted out and Arthur was "it."

He put his hands over his eyes and turned his face toward the trunk of the greening tree. The others scurried off to hide.

Art's voice could be heard halfway across the orchard as he counted, "One, two, three, four," and on up to "ninety-seven, ninety-eight, ninety-nine!"

Very loudly he shouted, "One hundred! I'm coming, ready or not!"

He whirled away from the tree, searching the orchard. But outside of Timmy, quietly curled up on the grass, there was not a soul in sight.

He tiptoed about, getting farther and farther away from the home goal. He peeked around the thick tree trunks, watching for signs of movement.

All at once he heard running feet on the soft sod. There was Ronnie, streaking for the home goal.

Ronnie touched the trunk of the tree and shouted, "Home free! Home free!"

It was too late to do anything about catching Ronnie. And then Dee and Emily sprang from their hiding places and raced home free, too.

"You're too quick for me!" Art said ruefully. "Guess I'm 'it' again."

But before he could begin counting once more, a girl's voice was heard on the road. "Yoo whoo! Yoo whoo!"

"That's Gloria Reynolds," Dee said. "Let's wait for her. Maybe she'll want to play, too."

"Who? Her royal highness, Gorgeous Gloria?" Ronnie scoffed.

"Oh, well," Dee said, "just because Gloria likes to be dressed up all the time, you needn't call her that. Besides, she is very pretty and always looks neat as a pin."

"She's too fussy for me," Ronnie said. "I'd just as soon she stayed away from here."

"Hush," Dee said. "She doesn't come very often, but when she does, you're to be nice to her, just as to any other guest."

Ronnie shrugged. "She lives only two houses away. She's not company."

"Yes she is," Dee said. "Be quiet now."

Gloria opened the side gate with a dainty gesture

29

and swished into the orchard. She was wearing a robin's-egg-blue party dress and patent leather shoes. Every hair on her blond head was in place, every curl just so. As she sauntered toward the other children she stretched out her hand affectedly. A gold ring with a large sparkling stone glittered on one of the fingers.

"It must be a piece of fake jewelry," Dee thought. "No girl her age would be allowed to wear a real diamond to play in."

"Hello," Gloria said, then stared at Timmy, leaning on his crutch. "Who's he?" she asked.

"A friend of ours from the city," Dee said. "Timmy Brown. Timmy, this is Gloria Reynolds. She lives down the road."

"Brown?" Gloria said, frowning. "Mrs. Brown's boy? Oh." She turned her back rudely on Timmy.

Dee's face grew pink and Ronnie's lips tightened.

Gloria held out her hand to the others, ignoring Timmy.

"What do you think of my ring? It's a real diamond."

"Honest?" Art said, crowding with the others to look at it.

"Of course," Gloria said. "The ring is very old. It was given to my mother by my grandmother. And before that my great-grandmother had it. Someday it will be mine to keep." She held it so that the ring glittered with diamond fires in the sun.

"You shouldn't be wearing it out here," Ronnie said bluntly. "See how loose it is on your finger. Suppose it fell off?"

"Pooh. It won't," Gloria said. "Besides, it's none of your business if it does, Ronnie Waters."

Ronnie turned away from her muttering under his breath, "It would serve you right if you did lose it."

The girls, however, hung over the ring, and Arthur, too. From the edge of the group Timmy's eyes were fascinated with the sparkle of the jewel.

"We were playing hide-and-seek, remember?" Ronnie said crossly. "Let's get going."

"Do you want to play?" Dee asked Gloria doubtfully.

"Oh, I might as well. I've nothing better to do," she answered ungraciously.

"You're 'it' then," Arthur announced happily. "The greening apple is 'home.'"

Pouting, Gloria turned toward the tree and began to count while everyone except Timmy scurried for hiding places.

"Ninety-nine. One hundred!" Gloria called out. "Ready or not, here I come!"

She searched for the others, but there wasn't a trace of them among the fluffy blossoming trees.

Gloria leaned toward Timmy. "Tell me where they're hidden," she whispered.

Surprised, Timmy stared at her. "I couldn't do that, Gloria. It wouldn't be fair."

"Oh, you!" she said furiously, stamping away from him.

She strayed too far from 'home' and the others dropped out of the trees and streaked to the greening tree. A very cross Gloria was "it" again.

"I don't want to play your stupid game any more," she snapped. "I only came to show you my diamond. I'm going home." She flounced away from them.

"You're lucky you still have it," Arthur called after her. "Next time you come you'd better leave the ring at home. You might not be so lucky again."

"I'll wear my ring any time I want to!" Gloria tossed her head. "It's to be mine anyhow. I can wear it once in a while now."

Ronnie made a face at Gloria's departing back. "I wish she'd stay away from here," he muttered. "She spoils our fun."

"Ro-nnie-ee! Dee-ee!" Mother was calling them from the side porch.

"That means dinnertime," Ronnie said. "Come on, Timmy. Are you starved?"

"I sure am," Timmy said, reaching for his crutch and scrambling to his feet.

Dee smiled at him and took his free hand. "Come along then," she said. She thought Timmy's cheeks were lots more pink now than when they first saw him.

Art and Emily said, "We have to go, too. Good-by."

The children waved to each other, and then Ronnie and Dee shortened their steps to fit Timmy's halting gait as they moved toward the house.

"I had a wonderful time in your orchard," Timmy said.

"Then come again tomorrow, why don't you?" Dee invited. "You're not going to school now, are you?"

"No," Timmy said. "I won't be going till next

33

year. The doctor says I have to get stronger."

"Then you can come every day your mother does," Ronnie said. "Or she can put you on the bus and you can come by yourself. We'll find games you can play with us."

Timmy sighed happily and tried to hurry—to tell his mother of their invitation, Dee supposed.

CHAPTER FOUR

The Airplane Game

BUT IT WAS three days before they could play in the orchard again, for it rained heavily for two whole days. It took another day for the ground to dry out.

On the fourth day, soon after the others came from school, Timmy got off the city bus. Dee ran to meet him.

"We're glad you've come today," she said.

Timmy was so excited that he tried to hitch along too fast and his crutch tripped him. He fell before Dee could catch him.

"Are you hurt, Timmy?" she asked.

"No. Not much. I guess I'd better not try to go

as fast as you and Ronnie. It's not easy to run on soft grassy ground with a crutch. That's one sure thing."

"Never mind. There are lots of other things you can do in an orchard," Dee said.

Timmy nodded cheerfully and swung along beside her, but she was careful to slow her pace to his.

When they came to the Harvest-Apple tree, where the others were waiting, Dee asked, "What are we going to do today?"

"Sh-sh!" Ronnie put a finger to his lips. "Look!"

The chipmunk was hopping along the grass, a piece of string dangling from his mouth.

"What is Chippy planning to do with that?" Emily asked. "Isn't he a cunning little thing!"

The children watched Chippie attentively. He kept hopping along toward one of the big roots of the next apple tree. Ronnie crept after him silently, but the others stood very quiet, looking on.

At last Ronnie spied the small round hole near the big root. Another of Chippie's doors! Sure enough, Chippy ducked down headfirst and pulled the string in after him. It went down much faster than the crust of bread, which he had been obliged to twist and turn before he could get it through the small hole.

"Isn't he the smarty!" Ronnie exclaimed.

The others joined him near the hole.

"I guess that string is gone forever," Arthur remarked. "Not that we care about a piece of string. But suppose Chippie had walked off with something really valuable!"

Timmy was examining the ground closely. Suddenly he shouted, "There's another little round hole. It must be another door to Chippie's house. I've been reading a book about animals since I was here last. It says chipmunks always have two doors to their houses—in case an enemy comes in at one door. They can run out the other."

Dee and Ronnie exchanged a smiling glance. They had been talking about this themselves the other day. But Timmy sounded so proud because he could tell them something he had learned.

"Aren't they smart creatures," Dee said. "I've always wanted to know more about them."

"I'll read up on them and tell you," Timmy promised.

They waited for a few minutes, but Chippie did not show himself again.

"He must have decided to take a nap," Arthur said. "Let's play something. Something special."

"I have an idea," Ronnie said. "Been thinking about it all morning. Wouldn't it be fun to play that the orchard is an airfield and the trees are airplanes? We could fly to far-off places and then come back and tell about what we saw."

"That sounds like fun," Dee said. "Let's do it."

"But how would we play it?" Emily wanted to know.

Ronnie was ready for that. "We would sit on a big limb in a safe place, each in a different tree, and close our eyes for a few minutes. We could imagine the places we were flying over."

Timmy's face shone. "I wish I could climb up in one of the trees and play that game."

His voice showed how eager he was to join in with the others.

Dee thought a moment. "We shouldn't play anything that Timmy can't do too," she declared.

Ronnie said, "Timmy could be the ticket agent. He could stay on the ground and sell tickets and call out when a plane was ready to take off."

"That would be fun," Timmy agreed.

"I'll run home and get some pasteboard that we can cut into tickets," Dee offered.

Timmy smiled. "I'd like that. And I could have time tables and tell you what time the flights were to start. I've visited the airport in the city and I know how things are done there."

"Good!" Ronnie said.

In a jiffy Dee was off to the house to get the pasteboard and shears and a pencil.

The sky was blue over the orchard that day. Most of the blossoms had dropped off when the heavy rain hit them, but the leaves had grown large and were thick and silvery on the trees. The orchard was beautiful in another way now.

When Dee returned she cut the pasteboard into small pieces for tickets and gave Timmy a pencil to write the names of places on them. He stacked them into little piles.

Ronnie and Art ran to the house and brought back a carton for a ticket window and a wooden box for Timmy to sit on.

All was ready, and Ronnie called out, "Each one choose the tree you want for your plane and the place you want to fly to. Art, you decide first."

"I'll take the greening tree and I'll fly over the Mississippi River. I've always wanted to see it."

Timmy searched among the tickets spread out at his window. "You'll have to fly to an airfield near a big city," he said. "Here's one to Denver." He handed Arthur a piece of cardboard with "Denver" written on it.

"Fifty dollars, please," he said.

"Oh. I forgot to bring any money. Can I bring it next time?" Arthur asked.

"No. You always have to pay cash for a plane ticket," Timmy insisted.

Arthur felt in his pockets. "I just remembered I have some money after all. Fifty dollars exactly. Here you are." He fished out a crumpled piece of paper from his pocket.

"All right. Thank you," Timmy said. "Have a good trip."

"Emily next," Ronnie called out.

"I'll go to New York City," she decided. "I'd like to fly over those skyscrapers."

"That's not a very long flight from here," Ronnie told her.

"I don't care. That's where I want to go. I'll circle the city several times," she declared. "Here's my fare."

Timmy handed her a ticket and she started for the Jonathan tree.

"Where do you want to go, Dee?" Ronnie asked.

"I was going to fly to New York, too. But now that it has been taken, I'll choose—" she hesitated a moment. "I'll choose Washington, the capital."

Timmy handed her a ticket to Washington.

"I'll fly on my favorite tree, the Harvest-Apple," Dee announced.

"The plane takes off in fifteen minutes," Timmy told her.

Ronnie stepped up to the ticket booth. "I'd like a ticket to San Francisco," he said.

"Oh Ronnie, don't go there," Dee pleaded. "You'll have to fly over the Rocky Mountains. The plane might hit one of the peaks and crash."

"These planes won't crash," Ronnie assured her. "The Apple Tree Airline always flies through safe."

"That's right," Timmy added. "We've never had a single crash as long as we've been operating."

Ronnie turned to Timmy, saying, "A ticket to San Francisco, please."

Timmy scribbled the name of the city on a piece of cardboard and handed it to Ronnie. "One hundred dollars," he said.

Ronnie reached in his pocket and took out five pieces of paper each of which he had marked "Twenty Dollars."

Now that they were all provided with tickets, the game could begin.

"Flight number two!" Timmy called out. "For San Francisco! Gate number six! Have your tickets ready please!"

Ronnie went to the pippin tree and climbed up to a spot where he could lean his back against the trunk.

Timmy called out again, "Flight twenty-five! Gate number four!"

Arthur went to the greening tree, swung up to the lowest limb and took his seat. The thick old branches really made very comfortable seats, and the trunks made fine back rests.

"Flight twenty-seven. To New York City!" Timmy called. "Gate six, please."

Emily ran to the Jonathan tree, climbed up to the lowest limb, a very big one, and leaned against the trunk.

Of the passengers, that left only Dee on the ground.

"Flight forty-one. To Washington!" Timmy

called once more. "Gate three-ee!"

"Harvest-Apple, here I come!" Dee sang out as she clambered up a fat branch.

When Timmy had given the signals for the planes to start, the children all closed their eyes and began to imagine that they were really flying.

It became very still in the old orchard after the planes had taken off. Timmy sat on the upturned box with a happy expression on his usually sober face.

But watching the others enjoying their make-believe flights became tiresome after a while.

"I might as well fly somewhere, too," he said to himself. "I don't have to be up in a tree to imagine I'm in an airplane. I think I'll fly to Plymouth, where the Pilgrims landed."

He shut his eyes and was off. In his thoughts he flew over Plymouth Rock and looked down on that famous landmark where the *Mayflower* had brought her passengers.

He was so interested in thinking about what had happened way back in 1620 that he was startled when Arthur's voice suddenly said, "My, that was a grand flight! But I'm back now."

Emily came down next, announcing, "I had a wonderful time over New York. It's such a big city."

Dee slid down from her "plane" saying excitedly, "I saw the White House and the dome of the Capitol. It was all very grand."

All had returned from their imaginary trips but Ronnie.

"I hope his plane didn't crash in the Rockies," Dee worried.

Although they could see him still sitting in the pippin tree, their game seemed as real to them as if he were off somewhere in the sky.

"He'll come back safe," Arthur told Dee.

But it seemed a long while to those waiting below before Ronnie began to stir, as if he were waking from a dream. He swung down from his tree and shouted,

"Wow! That was great! The Rocky Mountains were the grandest sight. I'm going to fly to California every day."

Now all the travelers began talking at once. But soon a familiar "Yoo whoo! Yoo whoo!" interrupted the excited descriptions of the different flights.

"There's Gloria," Dee said. "Come on over, Gloria."

"Oh—her again!" Ronnie said. "Why doesn't she stay home?"

Gloria sauntered in through the garden. Today she was dressed in an embroidered pink sweater and a wide, shimmering skirt, nipped in by a wide embroidered belt. Again she wore the diamond ring.

"You look lovely, Gloria," Dee said sincerely. "But you shouldn't wear such pretty clothes when you come to play in the orchard. You might snag the sweater, or tear the beautiful skirt."

"Oh, well, Mother will get me other clothes then," Gloria said. "I'm tired of these anyway. See, I have my ring on again."

"You'll be so-o-rry!" Arthur sang out.

"No, I won't."

"Well, just the same, if you're going to play with us, you ought to take it off and put it in a safe place," Ronnie advised.

"Don't be such worry-warts, all of you!" Gloria cried impatiently. "Besides, I have the ring fastened on for safe-keeping. See!" She showed them a thin white cord looped through the ring and then tied around her wrist.

"It can't come off."

She eyed Timmy on his box. He was gazing in admiration at her ring.

"It's the sparklingest thing I've ever seen," he said breathlessly.

"Yes, it's very nice," Gloria said carelessly. Then, "What are you all playing?"

"We're playing airplane flights," Ronnie said. "The apple trees are our planes. You wouldn't want to play that," he added hopefully.

"Oh, yes I would!" Gloria declared. "Why wouldn't I?"

"Those clothes—" Ronnie began.

"I told you I don't care what happens to them. Anyway, I don't like to wear jeans the way the rest of you do. How do you play this game?"

They told her. And then Arthur said, "You can have the Rome Beauty tree for your plane."

"All right. Now stop wasting time, the rest of you, and let's go places!"

CHAPTER FIVE

"It's Gone!"

"THE FIRST THING we must do is decide where we are going to fly this time," Ronnie said. "You tell first." He nodded toward his sister.

Dee said, "I'm going on a long flight this time. To London!"

"You'll be flying over the Atlantic Ocean then," Arthur said.

"I know. That's one reason I chose London."

"All right," Ronnie said. "Let her fly wherever she wants to. I'm going to South America, where I can fly over the Amazon and over the Andes Mountains."

"Whew!" Arthur whistled. "That's some trip."

49

"How about you, Emily?" Ronnie asked.

She thought a moment. "I'll fly over Spain. I might catch a glimpse of the harbor Columbus sailed from with his three little ships, when he started on his voyage and discovered America."

"That sounds interesting," Ronnie nodded. "And where will you fly, Artie?"

"To the North Pole," he replied. "I want to see the place where there's always ice and snow."

Gloria wrinkled her nose. "I don't care for any of those places. I'm going to Paris! I'll see the Eiffel Tower, and all the shops where they design clothes."

"But you can't see the fashion shops from the sky when you are flying over the city fast," Ronnie pointed out.

Gloria tossed her blond head. "I can imagine that I can," she retorted. "Anyhow, that's how I'm going to play."

"All right, all right," Ronnie agreed. "Do as you like."

He turned to Timmy, saying, "Write the tickets out for these flights. We'll soon take off."

Gloria was the first to pick up her ticket. When Timmy had handed her one for Paris, she hurried over to the Rome Beauty tree.

All at once they heard her call out, "Oh, dear! My diamond ring has caught on a twig. I can't get it loose."

Ronnie and Arthur ran to her. They found that the cord with which she had tied on the ring was caught on a small branch and was held fast. Gloria could not get it off, for she needed her other hand for holding on to the tree.

Ronnie tried to untangle the cord. "You certainly did a good job of this," he told her disgustedly.

Finally, however, after much twisting and turning, he succeeded in freeing the white cord.

"If I were you, I'd take the ring off," Arthur advised. "That cord will keep catching on to things all the time."

Dee agreed. "Yes, Gloria, you'd better take it off. You can put it in some safe place on the ground where you can easily find it again when you're through playing."

"No," Gloria said stubbornly. "I don't want to. It's perfectly safe with me."

"All right," Ronnie muttered. "Suit yourself. But if it makes more bother, don't blame the rest of us."

Gloria gazed at the precious stone, sparkling in a beam of sunlight. "Maybe I'd better take it off," she admitted reluctantly.

"Leave it with Timmy," Emily suggested.

Gloria climbed down from her tree and ran over to the ticket office. She started to hand the ring to Timmy, then abruptly changed her mind.

"No. I'd rather put it over there, on the stones around your old filled-up well," she said.

She flounced to the well and placed the ring down carefully.

"It will be safe here," she called back over her shoulder.

The others soon took their places in their airplanes. Timmy called out, "Flight twenty-four! To London. Gate number seven."

Dee ran to her tree, took her seat on a big limb and leaned comfortably against the trunk.

Timmy announced the other flights until all had boarded their planes. Then he gave the signal and one after another the planes took off.

The passengers shut their eyes and imagined that the planes were winging them up into the sky and far away. They tried to picture just how the places they had chosen must look, and to think how the views would change as they flew along.

Timmy sat very still at his ticket counter, watching the others wistfully. How he, too, would love to climb into one of the spreading apple trees and fly along with the rest of them! Maybe if he tried hard he could reach one of the lower limbs— But even as he thought of swinging up off the ground he felt a cold chill and remembered the awfulness of his fall a year ago. He stared down at his weak leg and shivered. No. He'd better stay put on the ground. He could imagine he was flying anyway.

He closed his eyes and flew toward Florida. "That's where oranges come from," he told himself. "Maybe I'll fly over some orange groves. They must be a pretty sight."

Only the chirps of the birds and the buzz of insects came to the ears of the travelers as their planes zoomed high into the sky.

After a while Ronnie opened his eyes and climbed down from his tree. "All right," he called out. "Come back from your long flights, everybody."

All the children climbed down from their trees except Gloria. They stood talking about how they

had enjoyed their trips, but she still kept her eyes tightly shut.

Dee called up to her finally. "Gloria! Come on down and tell us about your flight."

"Not yet. I want to circle Paris once more. Then I will."

They watched her sway dreamily on her perch. At long last she opened her eyes and swung to the ground.

"IT'S GONE!"

"That was wonderful," she said, stretching her arms.

"Let's sit in a circle and tell about our trips," Ronnie suggested. "You first, Artie."

Timmy joined the circle and they all listened attentively as Arthur began.

"I flew over the North Pole. It was wonderful up there, with everything white for miles and miles below me, except where there was ice. That looked bluish. No trees, no bushes, not a house anywhere. Not even an Eskimo igloo."

"Was there a real pole there?" Gloria asked.

"Of course not. The pole is a spot that stays in the same place while the rest of the earth keeps turning around. It's an imaginary place, like our plane trips are imaginary. But it was fun to go there."

Ronnie spoke next. "I flew over South America. I saw the broad Amazon River and followed it a long way. My, but you should see the great forests along that river. Mile after mile of green. And then the Andes Mountains. They are a marvelous sight, seeming to reach the sky. I could have leaned out of my plane and touched them, I think."

"Your plane had better fly higher than that next

time," Arthur warned, "or you'll crash into one of the peaks."

"I was careful," Ronnie said, smiling.

He glanced toward Emily, and she said, "My trip was wonderful, too. I flew over the ocean and came to the southwest part of Spain. And there I caught a glimpse of the tall monument that marks the spot where Christopher Columbus set sail early one summer morning in 1492, with his three little ships."

"Then what did you do?" Arthur asked.

"I turned around and came back over the ocean and reached here just as Ronnie was calling us."

"Now, Dee, what did you see on your flight?"

"I saw the city of London. I saw some of the high towers; and I'm pretty sure I caught a glimpse of the queen's palace and the Thames River and London Bridge."

"Now Gloria, your turn," said Ronnie.

"I flew over Paris, just as I said I would. I saw the Eiffel Tower and some stores where—" She glanced down at her right hand. "Oh! I must get my ring. Then I'll tell you the rest."

56

"IT'S GONE!"

She jumped up and ran to the stone well where she had left her ring. All at once they heard her scream.

"It's gone! My ring is gone!"

CHAPTER SIX

A Frantic Search

THE OTHER CHILDREN rushed to the well. Gloria was running round and round, searching frantically for her ring.

"I put it right here!" she cried, patting a flat stone. "Right here. Where can it be? Who took it?" She faced the others accusingly.

"Nobody took it," Dee said soothingly. "It must have fallen somehow. We'll help you find it. Let's hunt around in the spearmint beside the well."

"I'll help, too," Timmy offered, hitching over on his crutch after the others.

"You won't find it," Gloria stormed. "I know my ring has been stolen. My mother will be furious.

58

She didn't know I wore it outside."

The children stared at her, shocked.

"You mean you wore the beautiful ring that belonged to your great-grandmother without permission?" Dee asked. "Oh, Gloria."

"Don't you 'Oh, Gloria' me!" she cried impatiently. "I wish I knew what to do now." She began to cry.

"Stop crying, anyway," Ronnie said, "and hollering all over the place. Come on, gang, let's all look sharp and see if we can find that ring."

All the children began to scurry through the grass and the bed of spearmint. Even Timmy pushed the stalks aside with his crutch. Ronnie climbed inside the small hollow which was all that was left of the earth-filled well. There was no trace of the ring here either.

"Could someone have sneaked into the orchard while we had our eyes shut and stolen it?" Arthur asked, straightening up.

Ronnie shook his head. "We'd have heard a rustle in the grass. Besides, there wasn't anyone around but us."

Dee said, "The ring was so small, it wouldn't be

seen very far away—especially by a stranger. Maybe some little animal came along here and spied it. Remember the chipmunk with that piece of string? That's probably what happened to my ribbon, too. And that's what happened to Gloria's ring. I'm sure of it."

"We'll dig up the chipmunk burrow if the ring doesn't turn up somewhere else," Ronnie said slowly. "But there's no use in spoiling Chippie's house until we've hunted everywhere else first."

"We've done that already," Timmy said. "And the chipmunk could have taken the ring."

Gloria stared at him, her eyes narrowed. "You were the only one on the ground while we were in the trees—with our eyes closed."

"I had mine closed, too," Timmy said. "I pretended I was flying, too, even though I can't climb a tree."

"That's what you say," Gloria cried. "But how do we know? Maybe you took my ring. You certainly stared at it enough."

"Oh, Gloria!" All the children gasped.

Timmy's eyes were wide with alarm. "But I didn't! I wouldn't do such a thing," he protested.

60

"And I did have my eyes shut. I was flying just like everybody else."

Ronnie went to stand beside Timmy. "I believe you," he said. "You could play our game just as well on the ground as in the trees. Gloria, you shouldn't say nasty things like this to people."

"I don't care!" she flared. "Timmy is the only stranger here. He was the only one on the ground. And he knew where I put my ring."

"That doesn't prove a thing." Dee spoke sharply.

Ronnie gazed at his sister curiously. Dee was usually so gentle.

"Besides, the whole thing is your fault. You should not have worn a precious ring like that for play—especially without your mother's permission," Dee added.

"It's to be mine someday anyhow," Gloria argued. "I can wear it if I want to. And you're fine friends not to care about what happened to it. I won't ever come to your old orchard again—especially if Timmy is here. I still think he—"

Just then their attention was taken by a harsh sound off near the walnut tree. *"Caw! Caw! Caw!"*

"There's the crow," said Arthur. "Could a crow

63

have flown here quietly, picked up the ring and carried it off?"

"One did come the other day after a piece of aluminum foil," Emily remembered.

"I still think Timmy took my ring," Gloria insisted. "You'd better give it back to me," she told him in a loud voice. "Otherwise I'll tell my folks that you stole it."

Poor Timmy Brown was really frightened now. But he kept his voice quiet and firm as he said, "I did not steal your ring, Gloria. I didn't move from my place at the ticket office all the while the rest of you had your eyes shut and were going on plane trips. I told you, I had my eyes shut, too."

"Caw! Caw!"

The crow flapped to a nearby tree and perched there, eyeing the children. They watched him, wondering if he were the thief after all.

Arthur said, "I'll bet Mr. Crow's your thief, Gloria. Crows often pick up shiny things and carry them off to their nests."

Timmy's eyes brightened. "There is a crow's nest in the orchard."

"Yes!" Dee and Ronnie chimed in together.

"It's way up in the walnut tree," Ronnie added.

"C-couldn't someone climb up there and—and look in?" Timmy asked eagerly.

His voice seemed to say, "Oh, if only someone will do that, everything will be all right."

Gloria stamped her foot. "There's no use blaming the old crow," she said. "Timmy has my ring. I know it. You'd better make him give it back to me. You just better!" She burst into tears again and ran off toward her house.

The others stood there, staring after her. Around them birds were singing among the fresh green leaves over their heads. The sun was shining brightly. All was gay in the orchard—except themselves. The children glanced at each other unhappily. How could they find Gloria's ring so she would not go on blaming Timmy for its loss?

"We'd better do something," Ronnie said impatiently, "before that Gloria Reynolds makes trouble for Timmy."

Once more the children scattered to search. But it was no use. Before long they were gathered under the Harvest-Apple.

"There isn't a spot we haven't hunted," Emily

said. "I'm beginning to think someone did sneak into the orchard to steal it. Maybe someone followed Gloria over here! Maybe he hid until we were too busy with our game to notice what was going on. The way she kept flashing that ring, anyone could have seen it. Oh!" She clapped her hands over her mouth.

"What is it?" Dee asked. "Have you thought of something?"

Emily nodded. "The telephone man. They were working on the poles right next to the Reynolds' house today. Maybe one of them spotted Gloria's ring and—"

"Oh, rubbish!" Ronnie said. "You're getting as bad as Gloria. Suspecting everyone."

"I'd rather suspect them than Timmy," Emily said, her lip trembling.

Tears welled in Timmy's eyes. "I—I don't know what to do," he said, sniffling. "I wouldn't want my mother to know about this and worry."

"We certainly aren't going to tell her," Dee promised. "Don't worry, Timmy. We know you're innocent and we'll stand by you."

"Ti-mee-ee!"

A FRANTIC SEARCH

The call came from the Waters' house. It was Mrs. Brown's voice.

"C-coming!" Timmy called back.

He made his voice sound cheery, but everyone could see how miserable he felt.

"It—it's time for me to go home," he said.

The children crowded around Timmy, trying to comfort him.

"Don't worry," Dee said. "We haven't given up searching. You go home now, but we'll keep looking. There's the chipmunk's burrow if everything else fails."

Timmy brightened a bit at this. "All right," he said. "I certainly hope Gloria's ring turns up."

He squared his thin shoulders and leaning on his little yellow crutch, hitched up the orchard path to the house.

CHAPTER SEVEN

Mr. Crow's Nest

AFTER TIMMY HAD left, Dee said, "Let's go to the walnut tree. Maybe even with all the leaves out we can still see the crow's nest from the ground. Maybe the white cord Gloria had on her ring will show—if the ring is in the nest."

The children sprinted to the south side of the orchard. The walnut was a majestic old tree. Its great branches spread all around, but they were too far apart to climb. Ronnie shook his head regretfully.

"I wish I could get up there," he said.

"There's the nest." Arthur pointed. "Way up in a crotch. Almost at the top. See it?"

"Yes, we know where it is." Dee sighed.

68

"I know it's a crow's nest," Ronnie added, "because of the way it's built of sticks and twigs, not fine grass and feathers like most other nests. See the ends of the sticks showing at the sides of it?"

"Can't one of you boys climb up there?" Emily asked. "Maybe you could get near enough to see into the nest."

"I'll try." Ronnie shrugged. "But it's pretty hopeless."

The lowest limb was easy enough, for it was close to the ground. Ronnie swung up to it. But from there he couldn't reach the next higher limb. And he could not manage the trunk, because it was so thick that his arms could not reach around it.

Ronnie gazed up at the top longingly. "That's the first tree I ever had to give up," he said. He jumped down to the ground.

"How can we ever find out whether the ring is in the crow's nest?" Dee asked.

"We can't," her brother replied.

The children went back to the Harvest-Apple tree and sat down under it, completely discouraged.

Suddenly Dee jumped up. "The telephone linesmen!" she shouted. "That's the answer."

"Oh, no," Ronnie groaned. "You're not going to

start accusing everybody, too, are you?"

"No. Of course not!" Dee said, her words tumbling over each other in her excitement. "But don't you see? Telephone men know how to climb things and they have special shoes and belts and ladders! Maybe we could get them to go up into the walnut tree!"

Now Ronnie jumped with excitement, too.

"Dee! You've got it! Let's find the linesmen and tell them about the ring and the crow's nest. Come on, everybody!"

"They were working near the Reynolds' house," Emily reminded her friends.

The children pelted out of the orchard to the road. They turned toward the Reynolds' place, but the linesmen were not there any more. They were nowhere in sight.

"Oh dear. Which way do you suppose they went?" Dee asked. "Up toward the city or down toward the farms?"

"Which way was their truck pointed?" Ronnie asked.

"That way!" Emily said pointing east. "No! This way!" She pointed west.

"Make up your mind!" Arthur said.

"Let me think!" Emily pleaded. She shut her eyes, trying to picture the truck and the direction in which it stood on the road. "I'm sure," she said. "They were working toward the west."

"Sounds reasonable," Ronnie said. "I've seen them working toward the farm section. We'll try to find them that way."

"They may be miles away," Arthur suggested. "Maybe we'd better get our bikes."

"Good idea." Ronnie nodded. "Let's. And meet right here."

It did not take them long to get their bikes and gather on the road.

"Let's go!" Ronnie said, leading the way. "Don't forget to stay in line facing traffic. We don't want any accidents to add to our troubles."

They pedaled for almost a mile when Dee said, "Oh dear, I hope the linesmen didn't finish their job and go home."

The children slowed down in their pedaling.

Then Ronnie said, "I'm not giving up yet. Let's go a bit further."

And there was the green telephone company truck,

right around a bend in the road! The children whizzed toward it, almost piling up in their eagerness. They braked, stopped abruptly and leaped off their bikes. Two linesmen were working at the top of a pole. They stared down in surprise at the children crowded at the base of it.

"What's up, kids?" A big blond fellow called down to them.

"Please!" Dee called. "Could you come down? We want to talk to you. It's awfully important."

"We're rather busy right now," the blond man said. "Can it wait?"

"I suppose so," Dee replied, but she was so disappointed that the other telephone man said, "Go on down, Charlie. I can finish up here by myself. See what they want. Maybe they have a cat up a tree."

"No," Dee called. "It's even more important than that. It's a crow!"

"Huh?" Charlie had started to climb down, but now he paused. His face got red and he looked as if he were going to go back to his work. "Is this a joke?" he asked crossly.

"No, no!" Ronnie took over now. "You don't understand. Please let us explain."

"Well, okay," Charlie said. "But it better be

72

good." The hook-cleats attached to his shoes skritch-scratched down the pole and he thumped to the ground. "Now, spill it," he said. "One at a time!" as they all began to talk at once.

Ronnie was finally chosen as a spokesman and he told Charlie about Gloria's ring and how she suspected Timmy, and how valuable the ring was.

The linesman rubbed his chin. "That young lady could stand a good paddling," he remarked.

Ronnie nodded. "She sure could. We think her ring is in the crow's nest up in a walnut tree. But it's so high up, we can't get to it—"

"And you thought we could?" Charlie asked, smiling. "Well, we've had queerer requests than this in our time, eh, Don?" he hollered up to his partner.

"We sure have. I'm about through with this job," Don said, "and it's quitting time anyway. I guess we can help you kids out."

Don was a big, black-haired man with twinkling eyes. He, too, climbed down the pole.

"Where is this crow's nest?" he asked. "Lead us to it."

"It's in the Waters' orchard," Emily said pointing back up the road.

"You mean that apple tree place?" Don asked.

73

The children nodded.

"We know where that is. Come fall we always get our apples there. From your father, I guess, huh?" Charlie said.

"That's right, sir," Ronnie answered. "Dad always sells a few bushels to people who stop by the place. The rest of the crop goes to the city. We have wonderful apples."

"I know," Charlie said. "Wish they were ripe now," he added, as he and Don removed the leg braces with the climbing hooks on them.

"Here, we'll put your bikes in the truck and make better time that way," Don said. "Let's go, gang. No crow's going to decorate his nest with diamonds while we're around."

In no time at all they were back in the orchard, the truck parked close to the fence. The telephone men hauled out their extension ladder and put it up against the walnut tree. While Don held the ladder below, Charlie climbed up, fast as a monkey. Soon he was peering into Mr. Crow's nest.

"He has quite a collection!" Charlie called down. "Here's a shiny teaspoon. And here's a bit of aluminum foil. And a piece of colored glass . . . But I don't see anything that looks like a diamond ring."

"Oh, Charlie!" Dee wailed. "Please be sure about it. Please look again. For Timmy's sake."

"I'm looking, honey. I wish I could find it. It just isn't here."

In another minute Charlie was down the ladder and standing regretfully before them.

"Caw! Caw! Caw!"

Overhead Mr. Crow was scolding them indignantly. Protesting his innocence.

Dee and the others were on the verge of tears. Timmy was still in trouble, more so than ever.

CHAPTER EIGHT

Chippie's House

"I'M SORRY, KIDS." Charlie put a big hand on each of the boys' shoulders as he walked back toward the truck.

Dan had folded up the light-weight ladder and was already fastening it to the side of the telephone truck.

"It's not your fault," Ronnie said. "We do thank you both for coming over."

"Think nothing of it. We're glad to help. Didn't you fellows mention a chipmunk's burrow, though? Maybe that's your thief," Charlie suggested.

The children brightened, then hung their heads.

"We hate to spoil Chippie's house," Ronnie said.

"But I guess there's no help for it. It's not that we care about Gloria and her old ring. Losing it serves her right. But she blames our friend, Timmy, and she's the kind to make trouble for him. So we have to find it."

"I see," Charlie said. "Well, if we can be of any more help to you, you let us know. I'm Charlie Gates, and my partner here is Don Boyd. We'll be working on this road for a few days more. Now we have to be rolling."

"Good-by, gang, and good luck," the men said together.

With that the telephone men climbed back into their truck and drove away.

"I guess we'd better get at Chippie's burrow," Ronnie said, turning back to the others.

"There don't seem to be any other clues now," Arthur said.

"I guess we might as well do it."

"Look," Dee said in a hushed voice. "There's one of the orchard squirrels hopping along. Now he's running up the trunk of the greening tree."

"He has something in his mouth," Emily said. "Let's see what he'll do with it."

78

"He'll put it in his nest in the hollow of the green-ing," Ronnie whispered. "Say, maybe we'd better look into the squirrels' hollows before we disturb Chippie's house. They carry things away, too."

"Oh yes, let's!" the girls agreed.

"But be careful," Dee added. "Squirrels have sharp teeth."

"We'll wait until we know their hollows are empty," Ronnie promised. "See, there goes friend squirrel, out again on another quest."

The bright-eyed little creature scurried down the tree trunk and bounded away.

"Now's our chance," Arthur said. "Let's get up into the greening."

The boys swung up into the thick old branches, close to the trunk. Holding on to a branch above, Ronnie peered into the squirrel nest.

"Now I know why Mother sometimes says my room looks like a squirrel nest," he remarked. "You should see the junk collected here."

"Is the ring there?" Dee asked eagerly. "Oh Ronnie, is it?"

"Can't tell yet. Let's see, nuts, kernels of corn, big seeds, bits of grass." He sighed. "Nope. No ring."

"I guess squirrels don't care for shiny objects the way crows do," Dee said sadly.

Ronnie and Arthur jumped down to the ground again.

"There's another squirrel nest," Emily said, pointing to a hollow in the next old apple tree.

"All right, we'll look there, too," Ronnie said.

This time it was Arthur who peered into the nest. He poked around in it a bit, then shook his head.

"No. No luck here either."

"Chippie, here we come," Ronnie said. "That old Gloria Reynolds. If she hadn't worn the diamond ring, we wouldn't have had all this silly bother. We could be having fun instead," he grumbled.

Emily stared at her shoe tops. "My mother often says that when one person does something wrong, it makes a lot of trouble for other people. I think she's right."

"Let's get some digging tools from the barn," Ronnie suggested to Arthur.

The boys ran up the orchard path, but were soon back, lugging hoes and shovels. Arthur had a trowel sticking out of his jeans pocket.

"For getting into small places," he said.

CHIPPIE'S HOUSE

It wasn't easy to push the spades down through the tough sod into the ground beneath. Ronnie couldn't do it at first; but by pushing hard and changing the slant of the spade, he managed to dig up the first bit of earth. He started uncovering the burrow at the spot where the little round entrance hole was.

"Chippie must make himself awfully small to get in through that," Emily said. "I hope it's larger down under ground."

"It is," Ronnie answered. "Much larger. I guess he makes the door small so no big animals can get in after him. It's queer how those little fellows know how to do these things with no one to tell them."

The boys kept spading up the earth, digging deeper and deeper as they uncovered the burrow.

Suddenly Ronnie cried, "Snakes and humming birds! The burrow goes under a big root of this apple tree! I don't know how we can dig under the root."

"And it may be several yards long," Arthur said. "It may wind and twist, too. I've seen pictures of chipmunk burrows in my nature book."

"We'll just have to try," Ronnie said, stopping to wipe the perspiration from his forehead. "This sure

81

isn't an easy job," he said crossly.

"Let me dig a while," Dee offered.

"No," Ronnie shook his head. "Digging like this isn't for girls."

He picked up the spade and pushed it again through the rough sod. The sun was beginning to go down and they had barely scratched the surface of the chipmunk's home. There was a lot of digging to be done before they came to the real part of the house where Chippie's treasures were kept.

"Oh dear," Dee said suddenly. "Look who's here."

"Chippie," Emily said guiltily. "Poor little fellow."

The boys stopped working and glanced around. There was Chippie, sitting on his tiny haunches, watching them.

"He seems to be saying, 'What are you doing to my house?' " Ronnie observed. "Honest, Chippie, we don't want to spoil your home. You've Gloria Reynolds to blame for this mess."

Ronnie threw up another spadeful of dirt. Chippie whisked about and ran away. Ronnie threw down his spade.

"I'm not going to dig up another inch," he declared.

"Why?" Dee asked. "Are you too tired?"

"No. I could keep digging for hours yet. But I'm not going to turn a helpless little creature out of his home for any old ring belonging to Gloria Reynolds. That's why."

"It's not for Gloria exactly," Dee pointed out gently. "It's for Timmy. Remember? If this tunnel isn't dug out maybe we'll never be able to prove to her that Timmy did not take her ring. He did admire it, you know. More than the rest of us."

"Just the same, we all know Timmy did not take her old ring," Ronnie pointed out, "and I'm not going to dig any more."

"Neither am I," Arthur said. "Especially since we don't know for sure that the ring is in Chippie's burrow. It might very well be somewhere else. Somewhere we've not thought to look."

"Where?" Dee asked despairingly.

"Maybe it will come to us," Ronnie said, "if we put our thinking caps on, the way Mother tells us to sometimes."

As if the mention of Mother were a signal, Mrs. Waters' voice floated to them from the house.

"Coming!" Dee and Ronnie sang out.

"It must be dinner time," Dee said.

"I think I hear my mother calling, too," Emily Harris said.

"And mine will be soon," Arthur added. "I'll help put your tools away before I go," he told Ronnie.

"If only Gloria would be sensible and take back what she said about Timmy, we wouldn't need to hunt for her ring any more," Ronnie grumbled.

"It's too bad about Chippie's burrow," Dee said. "I wish we could put his house together again."

"Well, we can't," Ronnie said. "But if Chippie could dig it out once, he can dig it out again. I think we've only spoiled about half of it."

They started back through the orchard, walking slowly, the boys shouldering their tools. Dee glanced toward the center of their recent activities.

"Chippie's back," she announced. "And see what he's doing."

The small creature had gone to his burrow. His front paws were flashing back and forth, making the dirt fly.

"I think he is making another front door," Dee aid.

Emily nodded, then bent down to pull up her

socks. Before straightening up she reached out toward a green clump and picked up two sprigs.

"Four leaf clovers!" she cried, rising. "Growing right next to each other. I think that must be lucky. Here, Dee, you have one."

"Thanks," Dee said.

"We could use a dose of luck," Ronnie muttered.

CHAPTER NINE

A Light in the Orchard

THAT NIGHT, as soon as Ronnie fell asleep, he began to have nightmares. A great beast, surprisingly like the chipmunk, but grown into a monster, was chasing him all over the orchard—with a shovel! In his dream, Ronnie finally managed to run into the house and upstairs to his room. But then the giant chipmunk began to heave stones up against his window.

"I'll teach you to break up people's homes!" he kept shouting.

Bang! Bang! Bang! The stones kept hitting Ronnie's window pane.

Ronnie awakened, trembling. What a horrid dream!

A Light in the Orchard

Bang! Bang! Bang!

The sound was still coming from his window. Was me one—or some *thing* trying to get into his room? errified, Ronnie covered his head with his sheet. Ie was not awake enough to reason anything out. Jut then he recognized something familiar about the *bang, bang* on his window pane. Of course! How silly could a big eleven-year-old boy get!

He threw off his sheet and sat up in bed. *Bang! Bang!*

"Pooh!" Ronnie said aloud. "I'm not afraid of you. I know what you are."

He slipped out of bed and pattered to his open window. It was quite breezy outdoors and his window shade flapped hard against the glass. The pull cord went, *Bang! Bang!*

Ronnie adjusted the shade so the cord would not hit the glass anymore, smiling sheepishly in the darkness. Then he stiffened. Wasn't that a light in the orchard? He peered through the darkness. It was moving! As if someone were walking about with a flashlight. Who could it be?

"Charlie—or—or Don!" Ronnie said to himself. "They've come back to search for the ring."

He remembered how he and his friends had told

the men about the value of the ring. Maybe they weren't two kindly linesmen after all. Maybe they were jewel thieves. As he watched the light, Ronnie felt sure of it. Suppose they found the ring! Then no one would ever be able to prove that Timmy had not taken it.

Ronnie felt a hot anger rising in him.

"I'm going to chase those fellows off," he said. "Right now!"

90

A Light in the Orchard

He crept out of his room, so as not to waken the rest of the family. At his sister's door he paused a moment, then shook his head. No. Girls weren't much good at scaring robbers. Dee might cry and probably would be much too scared to be of any use. He wished Arthur were here. Between them they would show those fellows it wasn't healthy to prowl about the orchard searching for valuable rings that didn't belong to them!

Now Ronnie was downstairs. Through the kitchen ... He wasn't quite sure how he would chase the prowlers—but he would think of some way ... He stepped out on the side porch and almost dropped in his tracks, for a blinding flash, followed by a clap of thunder greeted him. Rain fell so heavily that it seemed as if great buckets were being poured from the heavens.

Ronnie peered toward the orchard. The light was gone! All at once he felt very foolish. Had he dreamed the whole thing? It had been an exciting day ... And suspecting those two nice telephone men, Charlie Gates and Don Boyd!

"I'm as bad as that crazy Gloria," Ronnie muttered under his breath. "I'd better scoot back upstairs before Mother or Dad find me down here and I have to explain to them. Won't I look silly then!"

He hurried back to bed and had just tucked himself in when his father came in softly to close his windows.

But this was not meant to be a peaceful night for Ronnie Waters. When he fell asleep this time he did not dream of giant chipmunks. Instead he dreamed of walking through a great forest. The wind was blowing through the trees, and as he looked up into the branches, he saw a huge gold ring hanging from one of them. A diamond, as big as a grapefruit was set into the gold. It glittered, brilliant as the sun, throwing forth sparks of green and blue and red, like a Fourth of July sparkler.

"That diamond is big enough to satisfy even Gloria," Ronnie said in his dream. "I'll climb up and get it for her. Then she will stop saying Timmy took her ring."

He grasped the great tree trunk and began to inch his way toward the ring. He could almost reach it now. He could touch it. He—

"Ronnie! Ronnie!"

Someone was shaking him. Ronnie opened his eyes in dismay.

"Don't," he wailed. "I almost had it!"

"Ronnie, wake up, dear." It was Mother. "My, but you were dreaming away. I'm sorry I had to spoil it, whatever it was. But if you don't hurry and get dressed, you'll be late for school."

"Oh." Ronnie sat up and scratched his head until his hair stood out in a touseled mass. "I had some dream," he admitted. "I wish it had been real."

Smiling, Mother left him. But it was a long time before Ronnie was able to separate the real parts of his night from the dreams. Even when he went down to breakfast he wasn't sure which was which.

On the way to school he told Dee about his dreams, and about the window shade, and about the flashlight moving in the orchard.

"I'm sure that was real," Ronnie said. "I wish I could have gotten out there."

"But who could it have been?" Dee asked, puzzled.

Ronnie didn't answer. He could not tell Dee his suspicions of Charlie and Don. In broad daylight they seemed pretty stupid. Instead, he said, "I don't know. And now we never will know, I suppose. After that rain we won't be able to find so much as a footprint of whoever was there."

In the days that followed, the children continued to play in the Waters' orchard. They kept a sharp lookout for Gloria's ring, too. After all, it might very well be lying hidden somewhere in the grass. Gloria never came near the orchard, however, and in school, when she passed by Dee or Ronnie or Emily or Arthur, she put her nose in the air and ignored them.

"It suits me fine," Ronnie said. "I hope she keeps this up."

Mrs. Brown continued to help Mrs. Waters with the housework, but Timmy never came with her.

"I don't understand it," Mrs. Brown told Mrs. Waters one day. "He seemed to enjoy playing in the orchard so much with your children. And I was so happy for him. But now, all of a sudden, he simply refuses to come out. And he won't tell me why. Do you think he quarreled with your children, after they were so nice to him?" Mrs. Brown asked anxiously.

"Oh, no. I'm sure that is not it at all," Mrs. Waters said. "They've always said the nicest things about Timmy. In fact, they said they wished he could live here and play with them all the time."

Dee was in the next room and could not help overhearing this conversation. She slipped away quickly, however, before anyone could question her. She longed to tell her mother and Mrs. Brown about Gloria Reynolds and her pesky old ring. But she wasn't sure that Gloria had told her mother about it yet. If Dee were to tell first, it might make more trouble for Gloria—and the rest of them—including Timmy.

But at the first opportunity she gave Mrs. Brown a note for Timmy. In it she said,

> "Dear Timmy,
> We all miss you so much. Please come to our orchard again very, very soon.
> Sincerely,
> Dee,
> Ronnie,
> Emily,
> Arthur."

She had told the others what Mrs. Brown had said, and the children had decided that a note to Timmy might do some good—especially if it had all their signatures.

Now they would have to wait and see if the note brought results. Timmy must come back to them.

CHAPTER TEN

Timmy Climbs a Tree

DEE AND RONNIE watched the bus anxiously whenever Mrs. Brown was due to arrive at their house. Two days later they were rewarded. Mrs. Brown got off, then turned back to the bus to help Timmy down with his little yellow crutch.

"Timmy! Timmy!" the children cried, rushing up to him. "We're so glad you've come back."

There was no doubt of his welcome. Mrs. Brown looked pleased as she hurried on to the house, leaving Timmy with the brother and sister.

Timmy smiled shyly at them. "I didn't think I should come any more—after—after what Gloria said about me. I didn't think you'd want me."

"Pooh!" Dee said indignantly. "That Gloria. She hasn't been here since that awful day she lost her old ring."

"And we're glad," Ronnie said.

"But—then it wasn't found?" Timmy asked.

"No. And we haven't heard a thing more about it. Maybe her mother doesn't even mind that it was lost," Ronnie said.

"Come into the orchard," Dee urged. "Emily and Arthur will be over later and we can play some games."

After that Timmy came to play with them regularly, and the matter of the ring was almost forgotten. But not quite. Every now and then a shadow would pass over Timmy's face, and the other children would know that he was thinking of Gloria's mean words to him. It bothered kind-hearted Dee that Timmy should be so troubled.

One day, in school, she stopped Gloria as she was about to sail past her.

"Wait a minute, Gloria," Dee said, catching at the other girl's arm. "I want to talk to you."

"I'm not speaking to any of you until you make that Timmy Brown give me back my ring," Gloria said coldly, pulling away from Dee.

"Then you haven't found it," Dee said. "I—I was hoping maybe you had . . ."

Gloria shook her head. "I even went back to the orchard with a flashlight once. Thinking the light might make the ring shine if it were in the grass."

So that was the light Ronnie saw from his window, Dee thought. That hadn't been a part of his dream. She'd have to tell him about it.

"But how could I find my ring," Gloria went on bitterly, "when that little thief you're such friends with has it?"

"Timmy doesn't have it," Dee said patiently. "Can't you understand that, Gloria? He's not that kind of boy."

"Oh, fudge!" Gloria snapped. "He was the only one who could have taken it. When my mother finds out about it she will make a lot of trouble for Timmy —and his mother, too."

"You mean you haven't told her yet?" Dee asked in amazement.

"No. She hasn't asked about it, and hasn't looked into the jewel box where it was kept."

"You should tell her," Dee said.

"When I do, it will be the worse for all of you," Gloria said. "Especially your little pet, Timmy. You'll see."

Dee turned away from the blond girl, feeling sick at heart. Poor Timmy. How could they protect him from any trouble? He was to come over this afternoon. She must not betray to him any fears she had on his account.

It was June now, and as soon as school was out, Gloria and her family would go to the shore for the summer. They would not have to be bothered with her until fall.

That afternoon after school Ronnie and Dee and Arthur and Emily walked down to the orchard together. There had been a class picnic, and they were all in jeans, ready to play.

"Boy, this is the life," Arthur said. "No homework and summer vacation only a few days away. Say, you know whom I saw from the bus today?"

"Who was it?" Ronnie asked idly.

"Charlie and Don. Working on the telephone wires again. I waved to them from the bus window, but I don't think they saw me."

"That's too bad," Ronnie said.

"Timmy is supposed to be waiting for us in the orchard," Dee remarked, peering through the trees.

"I don't see him," Arthur said. "Do you think he's hiding?"

"He never has before," Dee said. All at once she felt anxious about Timmy. "You don't suppose anything has happened to him, do you?"

She began to run, and the others pelted after her.

"Timmy!" Dee called. "Timmy! Where are you?"

"Here!"

His voice came back unexpectedly. But no one could see him.

"Where are you?" They all cried out together.

"H-here," Timmy said.

And this time his voice sounded quavery and scared, Dee thought.

"I'm up here!" Timmy called again. "In—in the Harvest-Apple."

"What!"

The children made a dash for the old tree and stared up into its great branches. Sure enough, there was Timmy, clinging to a branch high up, his face white with fright.

100

"Timmy! How in the world did you get up there?" Dee asked. "I thought you couldn't climb trees."

"I—I guess I can't. I'm too scared to get down," Timmy said in a small voice.

"But how did you get up there in the first place? And why?" Ronnie demanded.

"Look!" Timmy said, and pointed silently.

"Where?"

"Up here. At the tippy top of the Harvest-Apple," Timmy said. "See that piece of white cord?"

"Yes. Yes, I see it!" Dee cried. All at once she jumped with excitement. "Timmy, is it—is it—?" she hardly dared ask him straight out what was at the end of the cord.

The others saw it, too, now, and stood hushed, watching it—and Timmy, clinging to the trunk of the Harvest-Apple.

"No," Timmy said dismally. "It isn't. It's the cord all right. I'm sure of that. But the ring's not on it."

"Oh." Tears of disappointment filled Dee's eyes.

"But how in the world did you get up there?" Ronnie asked.

"I don't know," Timmy admitted. "I was playing in the orchard, waiting for the rest of you. Then I lay down on the grass—on my back. All at once I saw the white cord up there. I knew what it was. I just knew! I jumped up, grabbed a low branch—the one Dee always sits on. First thing I knew, I was way up here. I got to the cord—but there's no ring on it. Then I looked down—and the ground is so far away. Like when I fell from that clothes pole in the city—" Timmy began to shake with fright. "I can't get down," he said. "I just can't."

"I'll help you!" Ronnie put in quickly.

He swung up into the branches of the Harvest-Apple. But when he reached Timmy, he couldn't make the smaller boy let go of the tree trunk. He clung to it desperately, like a drowning person.

"Arthur, help me," Ronnie called.

Arthur shinnied up the tree, but he couldn't do anything with the frightened Timmy either.

"Even if we get him to let go, how will we get him down safely?" Arthur asked.

This made Timmy hang on even tighter.

"Get Charlie and Don!" Dee screamed from below. "Oh, please, hurry."

102

"I'm afraid to leave Timmy alone," Ronnie said. "He's so scared now, he might—" He didn't want to say the word "fall."

"I'll go," Arthur offered. "I saw the telephone men working on the road when we came home on the bus. You watch Timmy."

CHAPTER ELEVEN

The Mystery in the Orchard

NEVER HAD ARTHUR come down from a tree so fast. After that it seemed only a moment before he was in Waters' barn. Then he was speeding away on Ronnie's bicycle, down the road.

Ronnie kept talking soothingly to Timmy, while the girls watched from below, their hands clasped, as they hoped prayerfully that he would not panic and fall.

And then the big telephone truck was roaring up the road. Charlie jumped out almost before it stopped at the side of the orchard fence. In the wink of an eye he and Don had the extension ladder set up among the branches of the Harvest-Apple. Up he went, fast as a squirrel.

But the sight of the ladder seemed to give Timmy new courage. All at once he wasn't a bit afraid of being way up in the tree.

"I'm sorry Arthur had to get you," he told Charlie in a perfectly normal voice. "I don't know why I got so scared up here."

"Never mind," Charlie said, smiling broadly. "This reminds me of my first day way up on a pole. Don't tell anyone, but I had to be rescued! I just froze up there and couldn't make a move to get down."

"No!" Timmy said and burst out laughing.

"Yes!" Charlie said, and then his big arm was around Timmy's waist, guiding the little boy down.

All at once Timmy screamed, "Wait! Wait! Wait, Charlie!" He began to struggle in the big man's arms.

"Hey! Stop that, kid!" Charlie roared at him.

"Please, Charlie! *I see it!*" Timmy screamed frantically. "There it is! There it is!"

While the others watched, openmouthed, Timmy

107

stretched his arm and snatched at something on a thin little branch.

"I've got it! I've got it!" he shrilled hysterically.

The next minute Charlie was bringing him down to the ground, setting him on the grass.

"Whew!" Charlie said. "What a rough customer. Worth his weight in wild cats. Now, tell us, what's this all about?"

But Timmy was laughing and crying and quite unable to talk. At last he opened his hand and thrust something out toward Dee.

"Oh!" Dee shrieked, pouncing on it. "The ring! *The ring!* Timmy found the ring! I thought he was being light-headed up there, but he really did find it. Oh Timmy, I'm so glad!" She knelt beside him, hugging the little boy.

"I just happened to see it when Charlie was bringing me down," Timmy explained breathlessly. "There it was, caught on the branch below where the white cord was caught. I think Mr. Crow was carrying it away, but the ring caught and broke off from the cord and he lost it that way."

"That's exactly the way it must have happened, Ronnie said, nodding. "And with all the leaves an blossoms—and so many trees, we never saw it."

"But how you ever got up into that tree is sure a mystery to me," Arthur exclaimed.

"Now that the mystery of Gloria's lost ring is solved, explain this *new* mystery to us," Ronnie said.

Timmy tilted his head to one side thoughtfully. "I can't explain it," he said slowly. "Only—the doctor did tell my mother I could walk without my crutch—if I wanted to. But I was always afraid I'd fall. Then, when I thought about the ring up in the Harvest-Apple, I forgot all about my crutch, I wanted to get it so badly. So off I went. Anyway, playing in the orchard with all of you must have made me lots stronger than I thought I was."

Charlie and Don were staring at Timmy strangely. Charlie reached out and ruffled Timmy's hair.

"Don't try to figure it out too much, son," Charlie said gruffly. "Just be thankful for God's many blessings. I think the good Lord smiled on you today."

For a long minute the children were very still, staring at Timmy. And then Ronnie broke the silence.

"Well, now we must get this pesky ring back to Gloria. I hope I never lay eyes on it again, after all the trouble it's been."

"Me too," Arthur said.

The girls nodded agreement.

Dee said, "But in its way, the ring helped Timmy, didn't it?"

"Yes," Timmy said. "I don't even mind it any more that Gloria called me a thief. Let's go see her."

He stared down at his crutch. "I don't need you any more," he said happily. "Not really. But I guess I'd better use you a little bit, until I feel sure of my leg. And that won't be long!"

Timmy clambered to his feet, and stood there, barely leaning on the crutch. Everyone was smiling at him.

Charlie said, "We have to get back to our work. I'm glad everything's turned out okay for you, kids. Don't get into any more trouble now."

"No," Don added. "Because after today we're going to be working twenty miles away."

"Good-by," the children said. "And thanks! Thanks for everything."

They waved to the telephone linesmen until they drove away in their truck.

"Now," said Ronnie, "Gloria Reynolds, here we come. And we're going to make you eat your words!"

110

"Here's the ring," Dee said, handing it back to Timmy. "You should carry it."

He clutched it tightly in his hand, as if afraid it might get away and be lost again. The children marched out of the orchard, walking slowly, to give Timmy a chance to keep up with them. They were about to press the Reynolds' front door bell, when Ronnie spotted Gloria strolling in her mother's flower garden.

"There she is," he said. "Come on around this way, gang."

They hurried into the garden. Gloria stared at them.

"What do you want?" she asked unpleasantly.

"Just a few unkind words with you, smarty," Ronnie answered.

"Timmy found your ring!" Dee announced.

"Oh, so he's decided to give it back!" Gloria said nastily.

This made gentle Dee so furious, she rushed up to Gloria and stood before her, trembling with anger.

"Gloria Reynolds," she cried, "if you aren't the nastiest girl I know! It so happened that a bird found your ring that day and carried it off. The

111

string caught in the Harvest-Apple tree—and today, when Timmy was playing in the orchard, he happened to see it tangled in the branches."

"He did something very brave then," Ronnie continued, and told Gloria how Timmy had climbed the tree to get the ring. "We all saw the whole thing," he added finally. "Give her her old ring, Timmy."

Timmy stepped over and put the ring into Gloria's hand. Her face became very red. She was about to

112

speak when her mother walked into the garden.

"How nice to see all your friends," she said pleasantly. "I've been wondering why none of you have been coming over to play with Gloria. Oh, and who is this boy?" she asked, looking at Timmy. "I don't believe I've met you before."

"He's Timmy Brown," Gloria said faintly, putting the hand with the ring behind her back. All at once her face crumpled and she burst into tears.

"Why, Gloria! What's the matter?" Her mother put her arms around the girl and her eyes questioned the children gathered around them. "What's happened?" Mrs. Reynolds asked.

No one answered.

Sobbing, Gloria brought the hand with the ring forward. She opened her fingers and Mrs. Reynolds stared in astonishment.

"Your great-grandmother's ring!" she cried. "What are you doing with it, Gloria?"

"I might as well tell you the whole thing," Gloria said. "And after that I won't blame you a bit if you never let me wear the ring. Not even when I'm grown up."

Between sniffles, she told the whole story, includ-

113

ing her accusations of Timmy Brown.

"Oh, Gloria," Mrs. Reynolds said, shocked. "Timmy, I don't know how to thank you for finding this ring—and I can't apologize enough for Gloria's suspicions about you."

"That's all right," Timmy said shyly. "As long as that's all over now."

"I felt so badly about the ring," Gloria sobbed, "and so frightened about what you might say, Mother, that once I started accusing Timmy, I couldn't stop. Oh, I've been so miserable."

"And so has Timmy, I imagine," Mrs. Reynolds said. "You might think of that."

Gloria nodded silently.

"I am very much upset by your wearing the ring in such a foolish manner," her mother continued. "You are not to take anything from the jewel box again without permission from me. Do you understand?"

Gloria nodded, again.

Mrs. Reynolds turned to the other children. "You all have been very fine about this. I wish there were some way to thank you. And you, Timmy, especially."

"Oh, I got my reward," Timmy told her cheerfully. "The good Lord smiled on me!"

With that Timmy tossed away his crutch. He teetered for a moment on his uninjured foot, and then slowly, but very, very surely, he started to walk out of the garden, all by himself.

Ronnie and Dee and Arthur and Emily followed after him, smiling delightedly at the way Gloria's mouth dropped open with astonishment. Mrs. Reynolds, too, appeared quite puzzled.

"We'll explain to them some time," Ronnie said, waving a hand casually. "Right now we're going to show Timmy off to his mother."

"And tell her and our mother about the Mystery that *was* in the Apple Orchard," Dee added.

"Oh, the sports of childhood!"

sang Ronnie cheerfully.

"Roaming through the wildwood,
Running o'er the meadow
Happy and free . . ."

Soon the others joined them in their favorite song, singing lustily. And that is how the happy procession reached the Waters' house and brought two very much surprised mothers to the door.

115

After the excitement and happy tears over Timmy's ability to walk freely again had quieted somewhat, Mrs. Waters said, "And here I thought *we* had a surprise for you, children!"

"What? What?" Dee and Ronnie shouted, grasping her hands.

"What?" Timmy asked his mother.

"Well," Mrs. Brown began—

But Mrs. Waters continued, "From now on Mrs. Brown and Timmy are going to live here in the country with us!"

"Oh! Oh! Oh!" the children cried, looking from one face to the other, then at each other.

"Oh boy!" Timmy said, quite dazed by the good news.

"Oh boy!" Ronnie said, also overcome by the happenings of the afternoon.

"Oh joy!" Dee breathed. "It will be like having two brothers! Oh Timmy, I'm so glad. Now you'll never have to play in city streets. Our wonderful orchard will be your playground, too!"

THE END

BOOKS BY HELEN FULLER ORTON

A Lad of Old Williamsburg
Hoof-Beats of Freedom
The Gold-Laced Coat
The Treasure in the Little Trunk
Mystery in the Apple Orchard
Mystery of the Hidden Book
Mystery in the Old Red Barn
Mystery Over the Brick Wall
Mystery in the Old Cave
Mystery in the Pirate Oak
Mystery Up the Winding Stair
Mystery Up the Chimney
Mystery of the Lost Letter
Mystery at the Old Place
Mystery of the Secret Drawer
Mystery at the Little Red Schoolhouse
The Secret of the Rosewood Box
Grandmother's Cooky Jar